W9-CIL-910

For Aunt Patti,
whose spirit of friendship and humor
inspires me every day—AB

PENGUIN WORKSHOP
An Imprint of Penguin Random House LLC, New York

Penguin supports copyright. Copyright fuels creativity, encourages diverse voices, promotes free speech, and creates a vibrant culture. Thank you for buying an authorized edition of this book and for complying with copyright laws by not reproducing, scanning, or distributing any part of it in any form without permission. You are supporting writers and allowing Penguin to continue to publish books for every reader.

Copyright © 2021 by Ashley Belote. All rights reserved. Published by Penguin Workshop, an imprint of Penguin Random House LLC, New York. PENGUIN and PENGUIN WORKSHOP are trademarks of Penguin Books Ltd, and the W colophon is a registered trademark of Penguin Random House LLC. Manufactured in China.

Visit us online at www.penguinrandomhouse.com.

Library of Congress Control Number: 2021007170

ISBN 9780593384824 (paperback)   10 9 8 7 6 5 4 3 2 1
ISBN 9780593384855 (library binding)   10 9 8 7 6 5 4 3 2 1

THE ME TREE

ASHLEY BELOTE

Penguin Workshop

This is simply unbearable!
No space. No privacy.

It may be time to leave the cave life behind
and find some space. A space *just for me*.

COMMUNITY
CAVE SPACES AVAILABLE!
Flexible payment options
Great for hibernation
Located over the river
and through the woods,
obviously. ↓ AVOID
ALONE
HUNDREDS OF TIME!
ROOMMATES!

GET YOUR
SPACE BEFORE
THEY'RE GONE!

COZY CAVE WALL VIEWS
Move in TODAY!!!
1-800-ILOVECAVES

SEEKING
ROOFMATE!
Yes, <u>roof</u>mate.
I'm a bird, so
I live on the roof.

FOR RENT!
BIRDHOUSE
*No squirrels,
please*
utilities & cable
included! Call:
1-800-BIRDSRULE

SEEKING SOLITUDE?
BUY A
TREE HOUSE
TODAY!

MOVE-IN
READY!

*utilities
ON!*
*Fully
furnished!*

CREDIT CHECK REQUIRED!!!

Hmm . . . no roommates?
An entire tree that's all mine?

A tree just for me!
I think I'll call it . . .
The Me Tree!

My Porch

My Yard!

8

Wait . . . what? Who's in my tree?
It's not just me!

Squirrels?!
No wonder there wasn't any popcorn left . . .
I need a minute to myself.

Bees! You already make it hard for me to get honey . . . now you're disturbing my dreams! I need a good soak.

And now there's a manatee.
You've got to be kidding me—
that's my loofah! It's definitely
not just me in my tree!

17

IT'S NEVER,

EVER, EVER, **EVER**

JUST ME IN MY TREE!

I just want to be . . .

ALONE!

Dear B,
I cleaned
the
chimney.

THE ME
TREE

Can't you see?
THE ME TREE!

Finally.
It's just me in my tree.
No squirrels.

No sloth.

No manatee.

Bees?
Giraffe?

Is there
anybody there?

Nope. Just me . . . in my tree.
This isn't as fun as I thought it would be.

I think it's time for a change . . .

and I have *just* the idea.

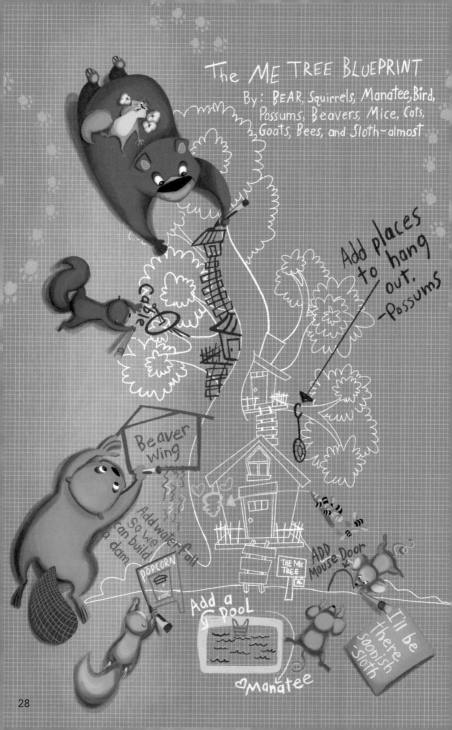

Let's turn
The *Me* Tree into . . .

The **We** Tree!

SATELLITE
DISH
SETUP
MANUAL
PART
2

TOOLS

Can we
get a
Dog?

Please